W9-BVK-768

Paco's Garden

by Lois Podoshen
illustrated by Buket

Richard C. Owen Publishers, Inc.
Katonah, New York

Paco and Abuela planted a garden.

They planted carrots in a row.
"When they have leafy, green tops,
we will eat them," said Abuela.

3

They planted tomatoes in a row.
"When they are big and red,
we will eat them," said Abuela.

4

They planted cucumbers in a row.
"When they are long and green,
we will eat them," said Abuela.

Paco waited.
He waited and waited.

One day, Abuela said,
"Tomorrow our carrots, tomatoes, and
cucumbers will be ready to pick.
We will eat them for lunch."

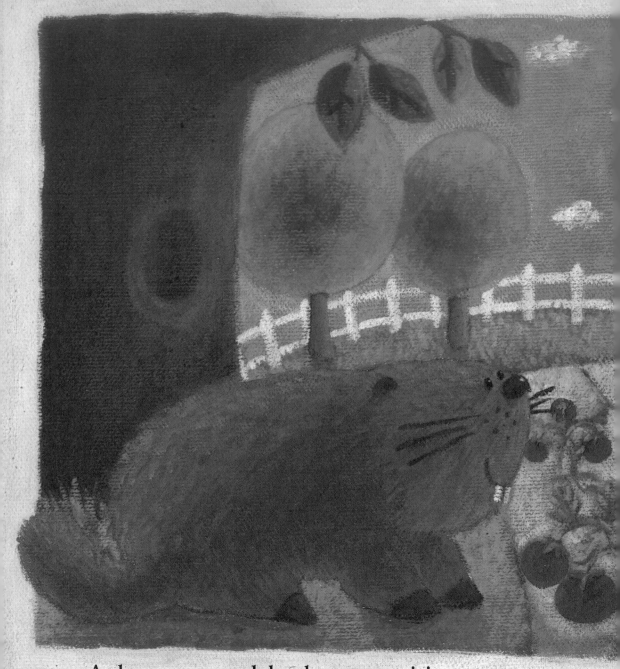

A hungry woodchuck was waiting too.

Carrots with leafy, green tops,
big, red tomatoes,
and cucumbers, long and green,
were his favorite things to eat.

So . . . "munch, munch, munch,"
the woodchuck ate lunch!